MONA
THE BRILLIANT

MONA
THE BRILLIANT

Sonia Holleyman

A Doubleday Book for Young Readers

For Benjamin

A Doubleday Book for Young Readers
Published by
Delacorte Press
Bantam Doubleday Dell Publishing Group, Inc.
1540 Broadway
New York, New York 10036

Doubleday and the portrayal of an anchor with a dolphin
are trademarks of Bantam Doubleday Dell Publishing Group, Inc.

This work was first published in Great Britain in 1992 by Orchard Books
as MONA THE HAIRDRESSER.

Library of Congress Cataloging in Publication Data
Holleyman, Sonia,
  Mona the brilliant / Sonia Holleyman.
    p. cm.
  Summary: To earn money for a new bike. Mona opens up a
hairdressing salon with disastrous results.
    ISBN 0-385-30907-4
  [1. Moneymaking projects—Fiction.   2. Hairdressing—Fiction.]
I. Title.
PZ7.H72476Mm   1993
[E]—dc20   92-23332
                                                               CIP
                                                               AC
Manufactured in Belgium
August 1993

10 9 8 7 6 5 4 3 2 1

It was Saturday morning and Mona's bike
had yet another flat. Mona polished the
rusty parts as Mom searched for the hole. Mona's
cat, Fang, was busy eating caterpillars.

"I really do need a new bike," Mona said. "A
brilliant new one."

"Your bike is fine," Mom said. "You'll have to
wait until your birthday."

But Mona's birthday seemed years away. "I
can't possibly wait that long!" she said.

When the bike was fixed, Mona and Fang
rode off. They needed to test it out. Mona
spotted her friends playing in the park, but no
matter how hard she pedaled, she couldn't
catch up with them. Their new bikes were just
too fast.

"Drat!" Mona cried. "I hate this stupid bike. It's plain as pudding. If only I had enough money to buy a new one."

Mona rode home dreaming of being rich and riding a shiny new bike. Then a brilliant idea popped into her head...

"We're going into business!" Mona told Fang excitedly. She found some paper and wrote "Mona the Hairdresser" in her best handwriting. Fang decorated the edges.

"This will draw the customers in!" Mona
said as they taped the sign to the front door.
Arrows pointed upstairs to the salon.

The walls were covered with drawings of a range of brilliant hairstyles, especially created by Mona and Fang.

"What lovely pictures," Mom said as she walked by.

Mona organized her hairdressing things. Mom's makeup and the cake-icing kit could be very useful. Then she got dressed up in her special hairdressing clothes.

"We have to look professional," she told
Fang as she tidied his fur.

Soon the preparations were complete.
Mona and Fang went into the garden to
await their first customers and to practice
their hairdressing skills.

The bushes looked really lovely with their trimmed leaves and the flowers were given an exciting new look.

Just then Mona's friends pedaled by. They screeched to a halt when they saw the sign.

"Can't stop to play!" Mona called out as she permed the daisies. "I have work to attend to."
Tina looked impressed when Mona told her about the new hairdressing business, and she asked Mona for an appointment. The others clustered around.

Mona checked her diary and booked them
all in for a restyle. "For a small fee paid in
advance, I will transform you!" Mona said
as she showed them into her salon.

"First I will shampoo your hair and then I will make you look beautiful," Mona said brightly. "No longer will you look like pudding."
    While her clients were choosing their hairstyles, Fang prepared the colors.

Mona was amazed by all the wonderful things she could do with a hair dryer and a bar of medicated soap.

"No one will recognize you," she told Tina.

Mona thought she had done a most professional job in brightening up Tina's hair.

"They're called streaks!" she said crossly when Tina complained.

The rest of Mona's clients looked on doubtfully, but Mona persuaded them to keep their appointments.

"I don't give refunds," she said firmly.

There were so many stunning hairstyles to choose from that Mona's clients were unable to make a decision.

"Professional advice is part of the service," Mona said cheerfully as she decided for them.

Mona and Fang created unusual effects
with Dad's shaving cream and some other
handy things from the bathroom shelf.

"It's the latest thing," said Mona
encouragingly. "It hasn't even hit the fashion
magazines yet."

Meanwhile, Mom was in the kitchen
practicing her karate chops and preparing a
snack for Mona and her friends. She was just
about to take it upstairs when Mona's friends
crashed past her howling and rushed out
of the house.

"They're not staying for lunch," Mona
called down from her salon.
But Mom came marching up the stairs.

"They asked me to do it!" Mona said indignantly as Mom, in her worst karate class mood, stormed into the bedroom.

"You're to return your earnings to your friends," she said, seizing Mona's bulging piggy bank. "And don't leave this room until it's clean and tidy!" she warned.

"All that work for nothing," Mona
grumbled as she began to tidy up. "Being a
hairdresser wasn't such a good idea after all,"
she told Fang miserably. "Now I'll just have
to make do with my old bike."

Just then, another brilliant idea popped into
her head. "What a brainstorm!" she cried. "If I
can't buy a new bike, I'll make one."

She carried down her hairdressing gear: the
dryer, the cake-icing kit, the shaving cream and
handy items from the bathroom, and set to work.

"This is going to be the best!" Mona cried…

as she rode away on her brilliant new bike.